John Sjoberg

HAZEL

& Other Poems

The Toothpaste Press   West Branch, Iowa   1976

Some of these poems have appeared in *Dental Floss, Gum, In The Light,* "*New York Times*", *P.F. Flyer, Search for Tomorrow,* and *Suction.*

Library of Congress Catalogue Data

Sjoberg, John, 1944-
	Hazel, and other poems.

	I. Title.
PS3569.J6H3   811'.5'4   75-30923
ISBN 0-915124-10-6   ISBN 0-915124-09-2 pbk.

This project was partially funded by the National Endowment for the Arts, and endorsed by the Iowa State Arts Council.

CONTENTS

7   Thoughts
8   3's Into 4's
9   A Sandwich
10   Plants
11   I Shut My Eyes
12   A Series
13   Valentine
14   Reality?
15   Walnut
16   Lord Byron Radio Program
17   Blue Tit
18   Arnold's Park
19   Who Knows
20   Short Poems
21   Gumball Fountain Duck
22   I Better Finish the Painting
23   Overalls
24   Fantastic Collection of Stamps
26   An Answer
28   Swell the Oysters with a Lovely Color
30   Wild Carrots
31   Pablo Anytime
32   Poem
33   (untitled)
34   Porch Window
35   Hazel

THOUGHTS

You have a headache Rimbaud.
You have an ashtray on your head.
You have a headache and you're sick.
The ward has gotten your nerves
To get up to get a glass of water.
You are really tired out, tonight,
And you're awake and thirsty.

There's a pipe and tobacco
on the mahogany table.

rattling leaves
wind blowing
music from a cello.

thin sensitive features
music from a cello
a lamp burning oil.

a slow drop of water
a second drop of water
a second drop of water
music from a cello.

a second drop of water
a slow piece of music
a raft, floating
a ball of string.

a lamp burning oil
music from a cello
the end of a long shaft
a slow piece of music.

A SANDWICH

Penguin Bread.
pumpkin.
pumpkin.
pumpkin.
Penguin Bread.

PLANTS

gertrude our geranium
i feel like i'm just dripping

feel

feel fine tonight

       wife & i up
doing things in the
          refrigerator
night

      ★

it
could be your wisdom teeth smelling
          things up

      ★

i laugh elephantine

   iceland
   iceland

i laugh elephantine

   iceland ho !

I SHUT MY EYES

i shut my eyes
and raymond burr
is sleeping there.
his black beard
grows on
into the next frame
and the next frame
and the next frame

and from one house
to the next house

his beards grow into the night.
on on and on.

A SERIES

1
"a cloud in trousers"
"rage on raw meat"
                    Mayakovsky

hold up your skirt and say "pretty"

2
a rage
held up his shirt
                while
a butterfly held open his lips.

his pretty lips
pulled apart   the shadows in a crevice.

the sweat of butterflies,
their elbows
            have begun to grow on trees.

3
a raging man
            held up his shirt,
as if two sweating butterflies
could hold his lips apart…

the words formed.

4
                    on a plate
          bacon
the two butterflies
                    sweated.
his lips were
pulled apart
(day had begun).

I'm too old for you, it's
8:30 tonight. Why not
make rainbows grey and
paint your face
the color of reflection?

I'm too old for you, it's
8:30. The village
has a horseshoe around
its neck and I'm leaving
for the city. There, grey
buildings reflect my dreams.

I'm too old for you, it's
8:30. I've heard a poet
rip his book apart. There
was fear in my heart. I
reflect. The shadow of my hand
makes a tic-tac-toe on the
polished marble floor.

I'm too old for you, it's
8:30. I'm on my
second cup of coffee. I see the
rainbow and feel like sleeping
all night and 12 hours
into the next day. Grey and
forgetful, sleep has all my
second thoughts.

because cannot hide the sponge's eyes
his sucking from color the spectrum of

this isn't what i want to write
                              but (blame it on
something) it's got me by the head.
                                   as if
where i look is where the sponge looks.
that blasted poet sponge. that blasted
head inside my head inside my head.
                                   to fight,
i suppose, takes hard-assed discipline.
                                        i must forget
the inspiration?   the tequila?   jose cuervo?

          N) No

Yes or NO?   who's sucking the uni-
          versal mind?
                         i ask myself, "is it the poet?"

then, where am i?   over in the bathroom drinking piss.
ober in der beastial pond.
                         is it true?
where turns the moon?   is it really white?

                         yes, the penguin particle my
self says yes.   it is w
                    h   r
               i   it is e
                    t   a
                    e.   l.
o above us above us above us
                         it's always there.
fighting with its intense radiation
                              the SPONGE.

WALNUT

chuck miller's book is coming out
miller's book is coming out
book is coming out
coming out
out.

"Guardian Angel"
Concept Backed

"sunday morning and i'm falling"

shiney shiney
shiney
        boots of
                leather

the last
cigarette
        is lit.

elements of the Mai Tai mix
elements of the rum
elements of the outgoing
elements of the cunt

"this is love in 1971"

and all the red matchbook cover says is:
"Earn Baby Earn!"

i am born as if to be born were rum's reason
and the dunes did not exist outside my eyeballs
flying from one place, landing in another, keeping
stoned: in my mind, the blue-eyed man in the tea-
shirt who laughs at nothing at all, because
it's there.

the train
the train

over at the Oatman's, under the oak tree.

LORD BYRON RADIO PROGRAM

consciousness relates long gravity or we
wouldn't have landed here we earthmen

our pages like paths over oregon territory
where we've never been but have senses for it

if indians come this way (being there before we
were) we will know this isn't england altho

words come from there being a tradition we don't
wholely ignore If chaucer were here too he'd

move over to her side we'd all laugh a little
as winter falcon would take his hand, laugh into it

and place it on her belly, big with john, the alien
from iowa 1971

but we've all held a mikrophone on this not totally
dark stage the intersecting cycles coming from the mill

throb until the great pomegranite appears
as a gift from iowa city to new york

9:21:71

BLUE TIT
for john hawkes

Absolute, freezing, eternity,
the blue tit.
Frozen words   nothing.
An expression   nothing.
A monument   nothing.

To just wait out
the feeling I have
(to shit.)

I am in
an absolute room —
no john
no place
when you have to,
no place. blue tit.

Books piled to the ceiling
Books half read
Envelopes ripped open —
one, with pink stationery
and brown ink letters
sticking out
sticking out — mouth & tongue

A cat's tongue
A canary pair of pants
Falling apart.

It was his birthday   again
More photographs were needed
He went
into the booth   The machine hummed

He was looking at it too much
"My hair is still wet" he said
                    the pillows
approached his eyes   He blinked
trying to shake them off

He soon would sleep   She
entered in   always entered
in
   "You are my lover" she said

"Go in front of the mirror &
comb your hair"
                    Johnny was lost
the vacuum-cleaner hadn't
moved   from its place
in the middle of the room

              this is early   Fog
enters   He combed his   then
went over to the bed where
she was lying   She opened
her mouth & closed it   Cues
for the little boy to pick up

The machine was finished   Johnny
walked out of the booth with a hardon

the lyrics,
        who knows the empty
ketchup bottle. the impossibility in late night hours.

who knows the record player!

who knows a peanutbutter & honey sandwich when
what you describe as sweetness is gone?
This is geography! this place , this room.
Burlington is a long street. while our lives
fluctuate.

the contours & tough lines of a bone.
our dog finds it worth chewing upon.

short poems, short poems
are the ones to write

write one long one
& you feel lonely all night long.
o mama, i've lost my green pen,
won't write another long poem
long as i live.

st. patrick's day is coming up soon
& i won't be able
to draw a good green picture
of you.

why should i ever write
a long poem,
if you are much better than you?

don't know why i'm upset
(obsessed?) with a duck, she
seems to have noticed me
& my nickles. across the square
the bus stops, she says she has
to ride it & i always give her
the fare. the other night, tho..
she was dressed in a green sweater
& nothing else.. which is more
than usual. as the trees passed
over the bus, a major highway soon
passed under us, on the town's lone
overpass. this is quite remarkable.

i talk about materials,
drink beer, & smoke cigarettes.
but it's yellow, Yellow
i need to add!

   hearin' the band play
makes it all add up.

     you forget the words, but
paints stay the same.

OVERALLS

mary wears them
light blue

     she even wears a gold
sweater underneath
    & no one can define how
she walks, when she is
wearing them.

     o, she carries it over
when she's in other clothes,
yet have you ever seen a farmer
in a suit?

    well, mary can play a flute,
either-way, but is most lovely

  in her overalls.

for bob dylan

I

somemore cigarettes, some buckhorn, some
   calligraphy
adis ababba touching his hat to his little

cigar, before he lights it.
   my cable from mama read "hangtight, i love you
So much!"   .

An albatross came in on a cycle, so you know
   we got luck. i read some of ted's poems to the
class, so we're off to a good start. infact
my cat has me completely baffled.

II

no real beginning. the beginning is now. did
you know baking soda can be used alot. i use
ultrabright, even so; yet there are lots more ways
of using baking soda. so i don't feel left out
without something to do, when i have (baking soda).

kissed mary goodnight makes the qt. of beer taste
so good! you know i have a little pipe looks just
like a toilet stool. kind of eggnog shaded towards
a little pink. the description never gets to the
fact that i can't use it. the glaze is the kind that
makes it smooth, so smooth i can not get a screen to
stay.

III

fanny farmer "turtles" are my mother's favorite candies..
while at the same time, my favorite matchbooks are
green cross. the relevance to this evening is that
i love my mother & i like to have a cigarette now & then.

IV

the red-brown fox quickly dashed over the wheelbarrow
but remembered william carlos williams .

why did george washington
try to kill himself?

it was morning and so george
had a cup of coffee. this
wasn't unusual. the ritual
of drinking a carefully poured
cup of coffee was
                        the beginning
of the day. he had red sox
on. this was a rarity for
revolutionary times. (red
dye for sox was not invented
until 1833).
                        george's cat
was playing in the bed-
room. martha had gone
for the day. she'd been
leaving the house rather
early these last few days.
she usually left with jerry,
the indian cook for the
washington family.
            (jerry was a bright young
brave, since he'd had an
education back in the early
days when he worked for the
measurement research corporation.)

                        the beginning
of the day. george looked out
of the house at the river and
all the maples that had
grown on this, his famous

plantation. george was re-
calling all the red-orange
maple leaves he'd picked
yesterday. it had been sun-
set then. their pet
peacocks had been strutting
all over the closely cropped lawn.
george felt good remembering
the peacocks. they always
reminded him of how terribly
immortal
          the washington
name would become. "ancestors
and descendents." said george
to himself in his

dove white kitchen.

(numer one) lavender penis your
beach or early poems
of God like before heroin was
created or n.y.c.
"zoomed" on to this northern
Continent

on Iowa grass or
birds we find an innocence light
vista lights home pizza

(numer two) last camel of the night
lavender laredo put a littlemore in the end
making it smaller and smaller and
more exquisite   clear green mug
didn't break on tile floor
make 5 packs between them   figured it out

ethnocentricity
like a liquid word

like roller derby

good thing apple is ringo in japanese
realistic   went right in and died light bulb

(numer three)   'slinger or
                  or jack's hillbilly not
                  good for that fan   escaped
                                    last night into
                                       electric world
                  in the morning the king found a turd on his throne

                                    golden
                               susan projects
                        glow little storys about men
                                                        mugged
                  at last after dream

(numer four)   milkweed returns remembers yearns
                  intuitively
                  for what darrell wrote forever

                  on this birthday of the earth

sometimes you should look
at the drawings on a can
of Old Style lager beer.
just because i've had some
tequila there are carrots
just within the edge of a
virgin forest. indians &
a few trappers have left a
barely discernable trail

carrots have a very hardy
orange. only the cabbage
holds on like the carrot &
everybody knows you need both
for good stews & soups.

instead of a bowl of chicken
soup right away, i think
i'll have some eggplant.

you are a man, the artist gazing out at the mirror
    & back thru your arms to the canvas
            then we, numberless years later
see you
        white blouse, orange fan of a tie!
        ..against that stroked, black background. i look
& when i look closely, see that the palette was
            the last thing you painted.
      Orange, orange!   ..is your palette
        Steady are your eyes .

The clock has a pendulum
The clock has a pendulum
The clock has a pendulum

Ole!

(UNTITLED)

We try not to touch so close to our hearts,
But the night's unavoidable mind has made us
Try to bind our lives with
Strings we cannot find.
Its deep placed calls of softness
Draw our threadful thoughts
To hearts that are not there.
This compelling conversation avoids
The definition of our indispensable sighs.
This silence is all we need. We hear
The heart of love, and wait to see
Its daylight dawning, and stay the day into eternity.

my head is green

the songs here, the bird songs

here & here & here

are my heart.

the tractor engine beats,

drives fall corn up into the granary.

my whole body can feel it. i wonder

if they'll take me into town

in a wagon.

i'll stop at your house

in a bushelbasket,

grinning from ear to ear.

for peggi pureheart

A.   rain outside and beer
inside
Jack went to a softball
game after work
              free fall
to yonder diamond
           Brahms
"sacred"

green little cylinders

      "news"
"eye"

B.   peanut butter and jelly
sandwiches
He's here again   the next
day
    Jaw
       "chase after them"
       "terrible" "i turn
to look at the clock

"sacred" Brahms "new"
easy on the syrup easy on the gas

   to get   off

my feet

C.   i'd like to have a pajama party
     Mark
     said THE MEPHISTO WALTZ is a
     good
             movie

     I'm past forty
                     "flash cards
     and all that"   gangman and all

     &
        all that: pestering us

     to photography   class

D.   the more the mam is merrier
     whatever
     colors you have in your mind
     Tom Jones
                   fishing for walnuts
     "one you love"
                     the night is still ahead
     A Journal
                 burn   almost gone
     in Iowa City
                             C-52

e.   Jesus is one
       the more men the merrier
      what if i
                   missed church
      but is it never lover

      jaw terribly
                     red around bottoms
      of his eyes
                    burned house
      that was on Gilbert   poets'
      house
              "eye"
                       flaguated   ring
      tumbles

              down

E.   Ted Berrigan is a
      poet is a poet is a poet
      swirls and i catch him

      smack him on the lips
      cucumber
                    Fugs
      toothes glowing in blue
      light

F.   "if i wait any longer...   world
     like white sands in an hour glass

     "kill for peace" what our age does
     while it eats 72 hotdogs whistling
     round
          the goalpost
                  "evening umh evening"
     Manchester, Iowa
             could have taught there

G. $2.83 is a party
     and games are played at energy
     levels
     Fugs have it again (broom)

     can't drink two beers, could he

     march the pheasants to Waterloo?
             of
     out   the foam
             of

H.   "this will have to be short
     one" "chimp come me come she
     come we all come together"

     A Journal
             toward salt lake city
     white sheep
            on the mountains
     bald eagle
            has other masters than
     white man

          "grey room"

should i go on?

I.   silence   except for the fan
      bleeding
      hearts after the storm

      i remember Donald Justice

      just before he
      left here
                He was sitting   tilted
      back on a chair
                        looking at the Iowa River
      and the sun going down

J.   Liz has got a little box
      short
      cardboard sides
      and a little plastic bottom

      space on the other
      side of fiction

      in clear places   on the paper
      i typed them on
                        originally
      autographs mean   a

      lot to me

K.   THE CORE
     leaks a little   baths to the natives
     spheres

     the imagination must keep up

     cigarettes steal me away   but he
     gave one to me

     itching   is almost gone
     teepee tepee   tip e

     not   if
           i   want
       to swim

L.   yes!   peggi pureheart gave birth to
     me
           almost 4 years ago
     we went to the space ship
     and heard him speak   to sing
     poems
               all of the elements were
     there
               II of us near the rear &
     way up
               time was spliced
     strobeascope like   as the
     blue ones   filmed & animated (almost)
     those on the stage

M.   speak about the time   everything was red
      the bed   the floor
                              i was in a danger area
      when i was born

N.   i swiveled about
                              with my eyes
      i could see ham and stuff
      get smaller
      and then larger
                              i even tried to
      eat my peas
                    We went for a walk
      no more cigarettes
                              looking for
      a sign
              Edward was almost
      king

O.   Tobacco & full time orderly
      lemonade
                    off to Wart and the
      whimple

                      as if i digested
      a whole calf giving it coca-cola
      only
              shave the neck &
      a little under the top part as
      well   ceiling it off blue
      lights in bathroom
                              wizard that
      i am
              flying out of the paper
              sack

P. Q. "We try not to touch so close to our hearts,
       But the night and the unavoidable press on and on."

          early work
          of poet   from out of
                               a tin box
          'til it just drys out
                               like forgotten mists.

          That is not the tale
                               standing on top of the
          bookcase
          surprising Craig & Jack
          toe touched
                       do i gotta have dope to write?
          ESCAPE HEART INTO THERMOS LAND

R.   "She is not any common earth
            Water or wood or air,
       But Merlin's Isle of Gramarye
            Where you and I will fare."

       let me love her   i do love to crumple
       her hair
       we are both having pangs of rebirth
       as the lizard eats

                          oowee   sparkle
       plenty sounds   beating beating
                          gallerys of insects

       his pants untied

S.   Back to the fort   dead soldiers
      "dismissed"   logs
      keep on going   we're going to
      finish off my pills
                              yes, tomorrow
      Wart
            "mama mia, that's spicy peyote"
      Tama is
                  eclipsing itself
      every year for two weeks   Long
      time ahead
                  even Steve Allen
      on the late "talk" show
                                    natural exercise
      to other planets   But they've got to
      come back   filters around their
      eyes

T.   Chinese walk
      He's the one who killed your mother
      walking on the eggs between
      planets
                  and i suppose i'm prejudiced
      because i saw nothing but a photograph

      MY LONELY VALENTINE
                        holds the trumpet down
      down a shady grove with all the birds mixing
      and telling each other of their delights:

          fiddles   "summer stock"
      being filmed there in Yugoslavia

      "he can't sing"   up & down

43

U.   wife:men   leading us as the moccasins
become smaller, subdividing
                              in the present
of four yrs. ago
                      heart change   only partially
magic margarita
                      we still go in for group therapy
Vikings   splash us
                      steadily   in mist

V.   nude   and do some touching
groups "i went to a lot of them"

red walled tunnel   under   neath   rooted future

W.   "through the darkness" Duke is
dynamite
harness my wet blown hair

   a
         flower due to
crystalize into yellow
snow
         have a pipefull
lint in mist
following the street to the pyramids
XY TO J + 5
Jack sleeps
                the geese crust
tangles in your toes   Bomb

X.   we are the last poets/the others
      will come afterwords
                          Sheer Mexico
      drops on his knees

Y.   anti-itch pills
                      the skin buds
       worked
       Happy as Harry as he sits
       by the lake of reflecting
                              orange yellow
       bright yellow
                   all over its body

Z.   7 & 7:30
      may there be peace with the baby
      who's been here before
      "do you know/ dontcha wonder"

      Mary, webs but there is   always a star
      "I am happy" on either side

                      on time

                          7:20 — 7:22:71

HAZEL

was designed by Cinda Kornblum; handset
by Steve Levine and Allan Kornblum; then
printed on Ragston paper in an edition of 500
copies by Allan Kornblum & a treadle-driven
Challenge platen press. Of this first edition,
450 were sewn and glued into wrappers; 50
copies were numbered & signed by the
author, then quarter bound in Japanese hand-
made Tomoe paper & cloth over boards by
the Black Oak Bindery.